Fancy NANCY

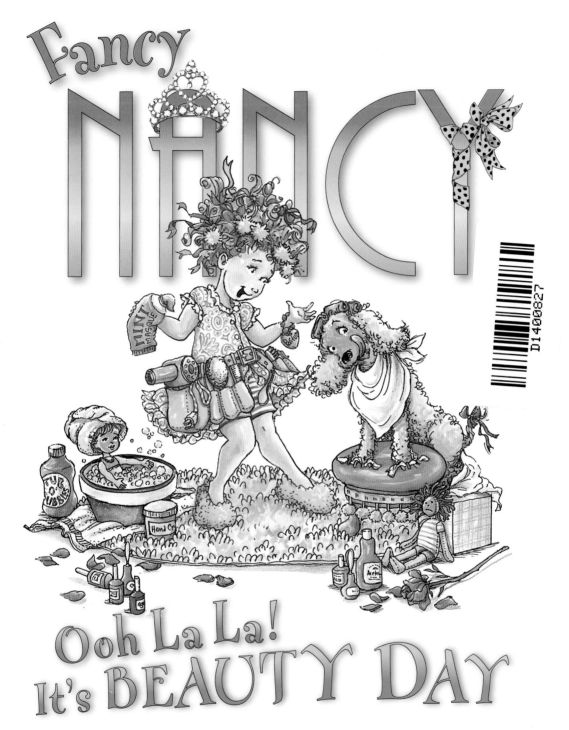

Ooh La La! It's BEAUTY DAY

Written by Jane O'Connor — Illustrated by Robin Preiss Glasser

HARPER

An Imprint of HarperCollinsPublishers

For Therese Burke, spa connoisseur and super-deluxe friend
—J. O'C.

For Sasha: a talented girl
—R.P.G.

When cooking or making crafts, it is important to keep safety in mind. Children
should always ask permission from an adult before cooking or using scissors
and should be supervised by an adult in the kitchen at all times. The publisher
and author disclaim any liability from any injury that may result from the use,
proper or improper, of the recipes and activities contained in this book.

Fancy Nancy: Ooh La La! It's Beauty Day
Text copyright © 2010 by Jane O'Connor
Illustrations copyright © 2008, 2009, 2010 by Robin Preiss Glasser
Crayon drawings by Suzan Choy © 2010 by HarperCollins Publishers
All rights reserved. Manufactured in China.
No part of this book may be used or reproduced in any manner whatsoever without written permission
except in the case of brief quotations embodied in critical articles and reviews. For information address
HarperCollins Children's Books, a division of HarperCollins Publishers,
195 Broadway, New York, NY 10007.
www.harpercollinschildrens.com

Library of Congress Cataloging-in-Publication Data is available.
ISBN 978-0-06-221056-2 (pbk.)

Typography by Jeanne L. Hogle
19 20   SCP   10 9 8 7 6 5 4
❖
First paperback edition, 2012

Bonjour, Fancy Friends,

My mom's birthday is tomorrow, and we're going to have a big family celebration (that's fancy for party). But tonight my parents are dining at a very posh restaurant, just the two of them. (Doesn't dining make eating sound so fancy?)

I want my mom to look gorgeous. So I am treating her to an all-expenses-paid afternoon at the Ooh La La! Beauty Spa. All expenses paid means it's absolutely free!

Love,
Nancy

Where is this super-deluxe spa?
Turn the page to find out!

The Ooh La La! Beauty Spa is conveniently located in our backyard.

Isn't it amazing how I transformed my clubhouse? (Transform is fancy for change.)

HERE'S WHAT YOU NEED

Ooh
♥ LaLa ♥
Spa ♥
Do Come in!

Pillows

Lots of colorful
towels and washcloths

Mirror

Flower petals
everywhere

Footbath
(our laundry basket)

Fashion magazines with
fancy French names

Lotions
(that's fancy for creams)

Relaxing music

Salon chair

When my client arrives, I say, "Bonjour.
My assistant and I are here to pamper you—
that means we are going to spoil you in a fancy, lovely way."

FANTASTIQUE FACE MASK

We start with a face mask. Face masks are pretty messy, so I wrap my mom's hair in a towel. *Voilà!* She has a turban. I add a pin and *voilà,* she has a fancy turban.

TRÈS EASY TOWEL TURBAN

Use a medium-size towel. (Thin ones work better than fluffy ones.)

Stand in front of your client. While she bends over, wrap the towel over her head.

Twist the ends together tightly and fold them back.

If the towel covers your client's ears, the turban stays on better.

If you are thinking a face mask is like a Halloween mask, you are mistaken. (Mistaken is a fancy word for wrong.) A face mask is a special cream with secret ingredients that make your skin beautiful.

Here is a recipe for the face mask. The secret ingredient is a banana!

FANTASTIQUE FACE MASK

Mash half a ripe banana in a small bowl. Add in about half a teaspoon of honey. Mash the mixture some and put it in the fridge until you're ready to use it.

My assistant places cucumber
slices over my client's eyes.
This feels very pleasant
and also keeps goo out while
I apply the face mask.

"Your complexion will feel as smooth as silk," I tell my mom.
(Complexion is fancy for skin—I love how there are so many
fancy spa words!)

The face mask stays on for ten minutes.

"Let all your cares drift away. Think beautiful thoughts,"
I say in a soft spa voice. Then I play relaxing music. I know
four songs on the recorder!

MARVELOUS MANICURE

Now my client is ready for her manicure.

First my assistant squirts lotion on my mom's hands.
Then I massage them. I rub her wrists and palms, and very
gently I tug each of her fingers.

"Mmmm, that feels so good," my mom says.

I don't mean to brag, but I do have the magic touch!

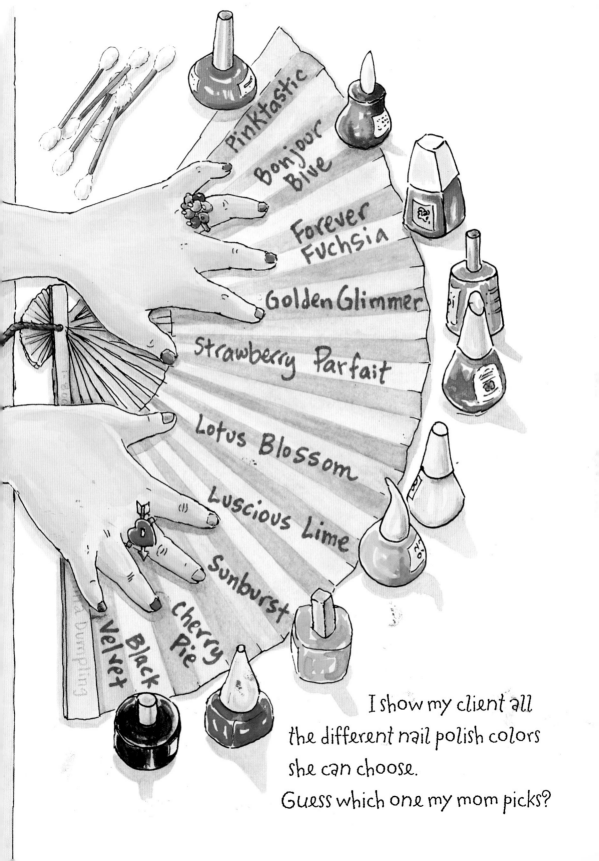

Pinktastic

Bonjour Blue

Forever Fuchsia

Golden Glimmer

Strawberry Parfait

Lotus Blossom

Luscious Lime

Sunburst

Cherry Pie

Black Velvet

Dumpling

I show my client all
the different nail polish colors
she can choose.
Guess which one my mom picks?

My mom doesn't like any of them!
She wants clear nail polish.

So Plain!

Pretty Nails
CLEAR

Our Motto:
Your wish is
our command!

I am disappointed, but
I don't argue. Here at the
Ooh La La! Beauty Spa, our
motto is "Your wish is our
command." (A motto is like
a rule, only fancier.)

HAND-Y TIPS

Shake the bottle of polish
before opening it.

Don't have too much
polish on your brush or
it will drip, so wipe your
brush against the lip of the bottle.

Start at the middle of each nail.
Brush from the bottom of the nail to
the top and then do the sides.

Use a Q-tip dipped in nail polish
remover to get
rid of mistakes.

Pretty Nails
CLEAR

We go outside now, where my assistant helps prepare a super-deluxe footbath. The tub is big enough so more than one person can soak her poor, tired feet. Heavenly!

SOOTHING SEA SALT FOOT SOAK

SEA SALT + 🍋 + 👜

Pour warm water into the footbath. Put in a quarter cup of sea salt. (Sea salt has bigger grains than regular salt.) Squeeze in the juice of one lemon. (Don't squirt any in your eyes—it stings!) Add lots of marbles. This looks fancy, and rolling your feet back and forth over them feels very pleasant.

PERFECTLY POSH PEDICURE

A pedicure is just like a manicure except it's for your feet. My mom doesn't want any polish on her toenails, but my assistant does. She wants her toes to look just like mine.

When I am all finished, she says, "Merci!" (All the employees at the Ooh La La! Beauty Spa speak French.)

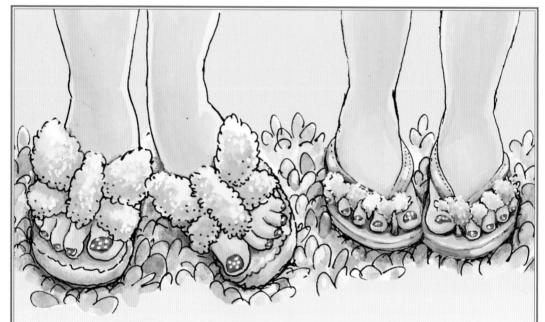

TIPS FOR TOOTSIES

Before you put on polish, slip your client's feet into flip-flops. Stick cotton balls in between the toes or else the polish will probably get smushed. When the polish is still wet, you can sprinkle on a little glitter for a super-deluxe fancy effect.

While everyone's nails dry, I perform several card tricks.

You're probably wondering, "Do all beauty spas provide entertainment for their clients?" The answer is no. That's what makes the Ooh La La! experience so special.

SPA CUISINE

By now we are all way more than hungry—we are famished. Spa food—or cuisine, as the French say—is light and good for you. Does an ice-cream parfait with chocolate sauce count as spa food? No! But a yogurt parfait does, and it tastes yummy, too. While we enjoy our refreshments, we look through fashion magazines.

YUM YUM YOGURT PARFAIT

Choose your favorite flavor of yogurt. Mine is raspberry. Put yogurt in the bottom of a bowl, add a layer of blueberries, more yogurt, a layer of banana slices, and more yogurt. Sprinkle some granola on top.

"Darling," I say to my client, "isn't this ball gown simply stunning?" (Stunning is even better than stylish.)

I can't wait until I'm grown up enough to wear an ensemble like this! I will look divine.

COSMETICS

(That's fancy for makeup.)

The magazines also show how, with the right cosmetics, ordinary ladies can look exquisite. This probably won't surprise you—my client does not want a total makeover. But she does let me apply some eye shadow, lip gloss, and blush on her cheeks. My mom is so pretty!

Before

After

My assistant gives herself a total makeover.
Frenchy is so scared she runs away, but my
sister thinks she looks beautiful.

Before

After

COIFFURE

(That's fancy for hairdo!)

Now my client is ready for me to style her hair. She does not have naturally curly tresses like I do. (Tresses is a fancy word for hair.) But I will give her a beautiful coiffure. No ponytail tonight!

I bought special styling mousse. On the can it guarantees "shiny curls with plenty of bounce." Guarantees are like promises, so that means this will definitely work.

I apply the mousse. (You say "moose," not "mouse"—it's French for foam.) I use a lot more than the can says because my client's hair is very straight. Also, it's so much fun to push the button—poof! Each time, a cloud of white foam appears like magic.

I make lots of braids. This is what transforms straight hair into curly hair.

My best friend, Bree, taught me how to make braids. She wears her hair in cornrows. She has twenty-seven braids!

I learned practicing with ribbons. Remember: Practice makes perfect.

Practice making braids with three ribbons in different colors.

Tape them to the edge of a table.

Cross the pink ribbon on the right over the purple one.
The pink ribbon is now in the middle.

Now cross the orange ribbon on the left over the pink ribbon.
The orange is now in the middle.
Pull the outer ribbons gently so the braid stays tight. Keep alternating right to left until you finish the braid.

Wrap a coated rubber band around the end.

While my client's hair dries, there's more entertainment.
I demonstrate (that's fancy for show) how to hula hoop.
Then I spell some very hard words, which my client
says is amazing.

Now it's time to take out the braids and see her
glamorous coiffure. "Are you ready for the new you?" I ask.

OH NO!

My mom's hair is horrible, hideous, horrendous! It's nothing like the picture on the can. "You can't go to a posh restaurant looking like this!" I say.

My mom tries to make me feel better. "I'll just put my hair in a ponytail," she says. "It'll be fine. It's not a big deal."

But it *is* a big deal. In fact, it is a HUGE deal. I want her to look gorgeous tonight!

There's only one thing to do. I call Mrs. DeVine. She used to be a beauty care professional. That means she worked at a hair salon.

Mrs. DeVine hurries over. She gets to work right away.

She brushes and sprays …

and combs …

and sprays some more.

"*Voilà!*" says Mrs. DeVine.

"It's *magnifique!*" I say.
My mom is so stunned by how beautiful she looks,
at first she cannot say anything.
Then finally she says, "Thank you. I mean, *merci!*"

Once my mom is all dressed, I say, "Ooh, I really want to give you one of your birthday presents now. It will look lovely with your new coiffure."

So Mom unwraps her new headband. She is so impressed that I made it all by myself.

"Au revoir," I say as my parents are leaving.

"MOM" HEADBAND

All you need is a plastic headband, three pipe cleaners in different colors, glue, and a few sequins. (Put sequins on *anything* and— *voilà*—it's fancy.)

Bend two of the pipe cleaners into tall M's. For the O, bend one pipe cleaner into a heart. Twist the ends together.

Glue as many sequins as you like on the pipe-cleaner letters. Then fold the ends of the pipe-cleaner letters around the hair band so it spells out "Mom."

Running a super-deluxe beauty spa is exhausting. (That's a fancy way of saying that I'm pooped.) But guess what? Tonight I get treated to some pampering and relaxation!

OOH LA LA!